Facing Your FEARS

Learning to be BRAVE

Jasmine Brooke

FOX EYE
PUBLISHING

Gorilla was **SCARED** of many things. He often felt **FRIGHTENED** about a lot of different things.

He got **SCARED** when he heard a **BANG**!

He was **AFRAID** of creepy-crawlies, too.

But being so **SCARED** stopped Gorilla having fun.

At school, Mrs Tree had a wonderful surprise. She told everyone that she would take them to the petting zoo.

Wolf was so excited. He loved all kinds of animals. Peacock couldn't wait to go. He loved to try new things. Panther jumped up to grab his bag. He was thrilled to be going on a trip.

But Gorilla shivered and felt very, very **SCARED**.

6

At the petting zoo Mrs Tree called, "Follow me! Lambs, lizards and even snakes! There are so many animals for us to see."

"I can't wait to pet them all!" shouted Cheetah. But Gorilla clasped his hands. Then, with a shaking voice, he said, "They look so very **SCARY** to me."

First, Mrs Tree stopped by the lambs. "They look so sweet!" she smiled. One by one, everyone fed a lamb.

"I want to feed them all!" laughed Peacock. "Me too!" Wolf chimed in. But Gorilla just held his head.

8

Then, with a wobbly voice, he said, "I don't want to feed them at all. They look far too **SCARY** to me."

Next, everyone visited the lizards. Some even held them in their hands. Mrs Tree said, "Aren't they amazing?" Giraffe and Panther agreed. "Wow!" said Cheetah. "I want a lizard for a pet!"

But poor Gorilla just said ...

"I wouldn't like a lizard
for a pet. They look far
too creepy to me!"

11

Next, it was time to see the snakes. Mrs Tree even held one around her neck!

Giraffe and Panther both took a turn with the snake. Zebra and Cheetah joined in too!

But when Mrs Tree turned to Gorilla and said, "How about you?" he squealed, "No Mrs Tree, thank you! Snakes look **FRIGHTENING** to me."

Mrs Tree could see that Gorilla was not having fun. He was not enjoying himself at all. Gorilla was so **AFRAID** of everything that it stopped him trying anything. How could she help him to join in?

"Do you know what I do when I feel **SCARED**?" Mrs Tree asked. Gorilla shook his head.

Mrs Tree smiled, "I imagine myself doing something brave, then I don't feel scared at all!"

15

So, very slowly, Gorilla stroked the snake. Then Gorilla gasped, "Wow, Mrs Tree, look at me!"

"Ooh, Gorilla!" sighed Zebra. "Weren't you **SCARED?**"

"Not me!" Gorilla smiled proudly. "It was fun! Not **FRIGHTENING** at all!"

At last, Gorilla had learnt to be **BRAVE**. If he ever felt **SCARED** again, now he knew just what to do.

Words and feelings

Gorilla felt very scared in this story. He found it difficult to be brave.

SCARED

FRIGHTENED

There are a lot of words
to do with feeling scared
and being brave in this book.
Can you remember them?

AFRAID

FRIGHTENING

BRAVE

Let's talk about behaviour

This series helps children to understand and manage difficult emotions and behaviours. The animal characters in the series have been created to show human behaviour that is often seen in young children, and which they may find difficult to manage.

Facing your Fears

The story in this book examines issues around feeling frightened when in new situations. It looks at how feeling scared about trying new things and avoiding unfamiliar situations can mean that people do not learn to enjoy new experiences.

    The book is designed to show young children how they can manage their behaviour and learn to be braver.

How to use this book

You can read this book with one child or a group of children. The book can be used to begin a discussion around complex behaviour such as learning to overcome fear and anxiety.

    The book is also a reading aid, with enlarged and repeated words to help children to develop their reading skills.

How to read the story

Before beginning the story, ensure that the children you are reading to are relaxed and focused.

Take time to look at the enlarged words and the illustrations, and discuss what this book might be about before reading the story.

New words can be tricky for young children to approach. Sounding them out first, slowly and repeatedly, can help children to learn the words and become familiar with them.

How to discuss the story

When you have finished reading the story, use these questions and discussion points to examine the theme of the story with children and explore the emotions and behaviours within it:

- What do you think the story was about? Have you been in a situation in which you were scared? What was that situation? For example, were you asked to go on a school trip that frightened you because it was unfamiliar? Encourage the children to talk about their experiences.

- Talk about ways that people can learn to be brave. For example, think about how you will feel if you try something new and find it is not as frightening as you thought it would be, and that you actually enjoy it. Talk to the children about what tools they think might work for them and why.

- Discuss what it is like to be scared. Explain that because Gorilla was frightened of everything, he did not try things that he may have enjoyed.

- Talk about why it is important to be brave and overcome anxieties about new experiences. Explain that by being brave and overcoming fears and anxieties you will gain confidence and try new things that can be enjoyable and fun.

Titles in the series

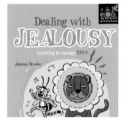

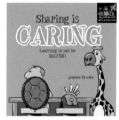

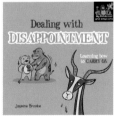

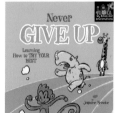

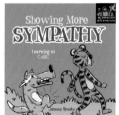

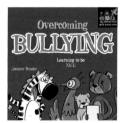

First published in 2023 by Fox Eye Publishing
Unit 31, Vulcan House Business Centre,
Vulcan Road, Leicester, LE5 3EF
www.foxeyepublishing.com

Author: Jasmine Brooke
Art director: Paul Phillips
Cover designer: Emma Bailey & Salma Thadha
Editor: Jenny Rush

All illustrations by Novel

ISBN 978-1-80445-301-8

A catalogue record for this book is available from the
British Library

Printed in China